last confession

last confession

Frank Rossini

sight | for | sight books
Eugene, Oregon

ISBN: 978-0-9839092-3-1
Library of Congress Control Number: 2020914451

sight | for | sight books
1395 Barber Drive
Eugene, OR 97405

First Edition
9 8 7 6 5 4 3 2 First Printing

Printed in the United States of America

Contents

PART IV

for Tom

we used to sit in Irish bars
counting angels on a pin
we tore the heart from every word
kept out from getting in
we'd argue muscle the height of fame
& who would win the pennant
the quality of the drink at the bar down the street
& the size of feet on the new tenant
& you'd ask how many eyes a baby would have
if both its folks were Cyclops
& I'd answer that depends on the time of the year
& which hand invented bebop
we'd talk Celt to the jukebox
drops dimes in our eyes
measure sorrow in glasses of beer
bought in rounds by the drunkest
of the mourners....

now I sing about high times
melt into stone
talk in tongues to a mountain stream
get way down to the bone yeah
way down to the bone

                        —from *high times*

last confession

Part I

It started with religion. And then the first
questioning of religion. That brought on
everything. You know, when I got to the age
where I started to wonder about things.
              –John Coltrane

last confession

> "I will drive boys
> to smash bottles on their brows
> I will pull them right out of their skins"
> > –from *Mary Magdalene* by Louise Erdrich

the first time I was seven the age of reason
one of God's lambs kneeling in a dark confessional
a small wooden panel slid open
a priest's shadowed profile fist beneath chin leaned
its ear to the black screen between us
"bless me Father for I have sinned
this is my first confession
I disobeyed my parents three times
hit my little sister once
I'm sorry for these & all the sins
of my past life"
"*ego te absolvo…* say three Hail Mary's"
I knelt at the communion rail & carefully
recited my penance

I grew older lied to my mother
stole a dime from my sister
used "bad words" I learned from my father
as he shifted the TV antenna on the roof seeking
immaculate reception

in seventh grade as the school strings rehearsed
their entry into *Aida*
a friend next to me in the trumpet section
showed with his hands
how a man enters a woman
the list of sins grew longer
impure thoughts   slow dancing
a French kiss

at 15 I touched a girl's breast
the sin of "petting"
not knowing he was opening a world
beyond my imagination the priest asked
"was she married"

at 17 they put me on a bus
with my boys school classmates
three days in the country
three days of prayers sermons
two silent nights in a single room
a cot a chair a small wooden desk
with a drawer where an earlier penitent wrote
about a mortal sin he imagined
committing with the local teenage girl
who served our tables at dinner

in the daytime we made the Stations of the Cross
the scourging the crowning with thorns   Jesus
his bloody face reminding us we were sinners
the young gray haired retreat master preached endlessly
the temptations of our flesh
how we should wrap our hands with rosaries
or wear boxing gloves to bed

& he told us the story of John & Mary
the perfect couple how they died John's car stalled
on the tracks moments after succumbing only once
to their "basest passions"
how they would burn for eternity
each moment infinitely longer than it takes
to empty the sea with a thimble
& how we could confess to him anytime
day or night face to face in his office

I knocked he sat behind a dimly lit desk
eyes bleary shoulders drooped
at the end of my sinful litany he broke

the unspoken pact of ritual
& asked "are you **truly** sorry" then leaning
his face to mine whispered
"Jesus **died** for **you**"   I mumbled
"I didn't ask him for that"
his face knotted he threatened
the loss of Heaven the pains of Hell
I was silent he sighed "*ego te absolvo*"
murmured a few more Latin words
& made the sign
of a tired cross

I shut his door sure
this was my last
confession

moving pianos

*for Eddie Leichtman, my stepgrandfather
& founder of Leichtman Bros. Piano Movers*

I was "the kid" the bosses' nephew   the boy
they sent to the bank with weekly receipts
my pockets bulged with cash checks & rolls
of coin as I walked the Spanish Harlem streets
before they became mean with junk   past Israel's
bodega Ramos' record store its tinny speaker
wired above the door   blasting the beautiful
sounds of Tito Puente Celia Cruz the young
Willie Colon   past the corner drugstore where
a thin young man daily imagined himself Dracula
covering then uncovering his mouth with a black cape
his eyes revealing nothing   on the way back
I stopped at the hot dog cart & fell in love
with the Puerto Rican girls   their eyes black
as the beads of my mother's rosary their tongue
sweet as Latin

at 12 I was the office help
adding long columns of numbers in the account books
till I became fast as my uncle   calculating
the sums in a small place just above my heart
I could **feel** if I was right   I was the janitor
sweeping the concrete aisles between the pianos
I couldn't lift   my arms thin adolescent wires
used to hours of basketball but not to music's
weight   in the slow afternoons in the back
of the warehouse I'd try to lift one end
of a spinet imagining myself Murphy   cigarette
dangling from a corner of his mouth   laughing
at insults tossed between "the men"   blue outlined
women writhing on his forearms as he raised a piano

with a slight straightening of his bent knees
then dropped his pants to prove he had eyes
tattooed on the cheeks of his ass

the next year I smoked three packs a day
& could hold my end of a Wurlitzer
I learned how to "dutch" a piano
onto the truck's tailgate   throw one end onto a
canvas pad the other into the air turn & drop it
in my partner's hands slip a wooden roller under
its sliding board crouch at the low end & push
I learned the ties to secure it to the truck
how to pad where to place the wooden chocks
to save the legs how to take it up stairs
around corners through doorways made for the thin
I learned how to carry a baby grand an organ
an eight-foot Steinway concert into houses
where Big Henny said "the only thing they know
how to play is the fuckin' radio"

& I learned about "the men"
Butch the shop steward who did everything
by the book & always wore a spotless uniform
of heavy cotton shirt & pants & read the racing forms
between stops   Preacher who had a storefront church
in Harlem & would caution me that the men's harsh words
about one uncle were nothing   but they were the truth
Russell whose solemn strength stopped the racist
jokes   he was shot resting on his stoop one Friday
evening for his weekly pay   Benny who lived in his
unpaidfor Cadillac & always offered to balance
the keyboard when there was an upright to "hump" 4
stories   Murphy who lived on the edge
whose back was a tattooed map of navy ports
& his face the path of coming disasters
who sang & played an old upright as it slid
from the back of the truck into traffic

& I learned about my uncles the bosses   Howard
the career military man squeezed out
when they decided they wanted the degreed
to lead the uneducated into slaughter   his motto
there was always work
& if there wasn't he would make some
moving stacks of pianos from one side of the warehouse
to the other in the heat which covered us
like dusty burlap & George my uncle of the big heart
the one they'd ask for an advance a day off some time
to get things straight   who'd buy beers
on hot Friday afternoons & send the men home
early   whose heart burst from too much
smoke & food & sweet times

I learned how the day could break
a man with its labor turn on him
like a dog slipping back into wildness
how fragile the back & bone hand & shoulder
how the strength of the whole can bring
down each part   I learned how to be
the weight I carried   to move
like the masters   I learned the art
of work

learning to dance

my older sister taught me how to dance
in the basement   stack of 45's
by the record player at first
no music my right hand in her left
left hand on her shoulder her right
on my waist she counted
the steps   slowly then faster
faster till she dropped
the needle on *Tequila*

by week's end I took the lead
unwound her from my left hand
passed her behind my back caught her
with my right twirled her twice & dipped her
then began again   *At the Hop*
Rockin' Robin goodness gracious
Great Balls of Fire

no one taught me how to slow dance
I spied on my sister & her girl friends
dancing with one another making fun
of how the boys moved clumsily
as they tried to get close

I would be cooler use my turns my spins
& if the lights were low enough
& I had just a little luck   *In the Still of the Night*
I might dip in
to a kiss

sex ed

my father knelt by his side of the motel bed
made the sign of the cross & prayed
silently   we were visiting his youngest brother
at a military base   my father & I
in one room my mother & three sisters
in another   I was twelve
I had never slept in the same bed with my father
he finished his prayers & asked
if I had questions about girls I had many
I said no   he said OK ask me
if you ever do   we never spoke about it
again

freshman year an all boys high school
sex ed two maybe three
forty-five minute classes our teacher
a nervous young priest passed out vocabulary sheets – penis scrotum
testicles testes erection sperm ejaculation
vagina uterus fallopian tubes
ovary ova intercourse fertilization fetus –
& two minimal drawings – a man a woman faceless
hairless labeled with appropriate vocabulary –
there would be lectures with limited time for questions

after class we joked about the words
pretended we knew more
someone rubbed the two drawings together face to face
he used different words   meaningless
when I heard them in a storefront two summers before
from the older boys with their slick backed hair cigarettes
& tough voices as we folded our newspapers for morning delivery

at home my older sister questioned me
I showed her the drawings explained the vocabulary

she said "I didn't know that
or that"

what I needed to learn I learned
later   on my own

Brooklyn girls

moon waxing   wife asleep
I read a book of Brooklyn poems everything
from Whitman's democratic hosannahs to a teenager's post-
coital prayer   in high school
I went out with two Brooklyn girls one
a blind date on a boat
ride to Bear Mountain an Italian
friend of a friend's
girlfriend we liked
each other but lived
three trains apart the other
a Polish girl I met at a Sunday
afternoon teen dance in the ballroom
of a Catholic hospital
we kissed pressed
our clothed bodies into one
another for an hour in her darkened
doorway while her mother watched
TV inside
but it was two trains a bus & a long
painful walk home
in the cold

I went to Coney Island once
with some friends to meet
girls who never
showed up   all
our money gone
on beer a cop caught me
last one jumping the subway turnstile
he gave me a ticket
a court appearance & a token
to get home

"Brooklyn" it's from the Dutch
"gebroken landt" "broken land"
a small piece of a long
island in memory's moon-
drenched sea

Brooklyn

learning to box

for my grandfather Giorgio Rosini (1880 – 1946)

my friend Stephen got boxing gloves
one Christmas   ten years old we laced them up
it was over in a minute   five jabs
& a straight right to my nose that night
I asked my father to teach me
how to box

hands up protect your face
elbows in   guard your body
left foot forward right foot back
turn your body slightly
crouch make a smaller target
he showed me the jab the straight right
the hook the uppercut how to feint
with my head strike with one hand
follow with the other & move
move move make him chase you   practice
with your shadow

Friday nights we watched the fights
brought to us by razors & beer
my father & step grandfather smoking cigars
drinking whiskey as the heavyweights
Rocky Marciano & Jersey Joe Walcott plod
& pounded till Jersey Joe tired fell
to a single knockout punch
or the middle & welterweights smaller men
my father's size thick trunks fast hands
grizzled faces   going 10
12 15 rounds first one then the other
rocked & wobbled their noses bloodied brows split
sometimes a draw at the end

as they leaned
into each other's flesh   exhausted

one night Emile Griffith from the Virgin Islands
versus the Cuban Benny "Kid" Paret
bad blood before the fight   Paret taunted Griffith
called him *maricon* a fag a queer
Griffith drove Paret into a corner relentless
punches to his head till Paret sagged
arms tangled in the ropes
the referee behind Griffith couldn't see
Griffith punching as he was taught
till his opponent dropped the referee
finally dragged Griffith off raised his hand
Benny "Kid" Paret limp unconscious
slid from the ropes

after my father died I asked his brother
how my father learned to box
he showed me a yellowed newspaper photo my grandfather
a young man
hands up elbows in   at the beginning
of a new century a student
of "The Sweet Science"   ready to fight
for his life

the day John Coltrane died   July 17 1967

the day before John Coltrane died
Robert Hunt a young Black soldier on leave
died in the Cairo Illinois jail
the police report stated he was stopped
for a faulty tail light
arrested for disorderly conduct
when he became verbally aggressive

the report stated that Robert Hunt's cellmate
called for a jailor shortly after midnight
that the cellmate saw Robert Hunt hang himself
by his own t-shirt from wire mesh
nailed to the cell ceiling
that the coroner verified the cause of death
asphyxiation by hanging
directed the body be sent
to a funeral home to be embalmed
then returned to family

the undertaker saw bruises on Hunt's body
called the local NAACP president
he viewed the body
confirmed the undertaker's observations
visited the jail cell
tried to hang from the wire mesh
his weight pulled the mesh loose
he asked to talk to the cellmate
was told he had been released
asked for his name
they couldn't find the records
he requested an investigation
his request was denied

the day John Coltrane died fires burned in Cairo
residents protested in the streets
some were beaten & jailed
the police chief called for the National Guard
deputized a group of white citizens
they named themselves "The White Hats"
the head of the local NAACP demanded a federal probe
J. Edgar Hoover ordered the FBI to investigate
the protest leaders
Robert Hunt's case was closed
the protests continued for six years

student teaching Roxbury

a week before the term began
they gave my master teacher a new job
they gave me her two classes
7th & 8th grade language arts fifty students
on my own

in time I learned
to have two lesson plans one in plain view
the required curriculum one hidden
for teaching the writers I was learning
to read   Langston Hughes Gwendolyn Brooks
Richard Wright

once a month a supervisor from downtown
evaluated my teaching "your tie was pulled down
your top shirt button open the window shades
were not all at the same level"

when Martin Luther King Jr. was assassinated
they locked the school down   I asked
to bring a neighborhood group to talk with the students
they said not here   in the park
across the street   once

& they came
with drums dance
& poetry

at the year's end my supervisor told me
"don't bother to apply for a job
in this city"

the wedding reception

I walk in to a long table
of groaning platters   fancy hors d'oeuvres
arranged around a sculptured swan of ice
an open bar   grandparents parents aunts uncles cousins
fidgety kids people from the neighborhood the priest
who put me to sleep with his droning line
by line explication of St.Paul's Epistle
on Love before he declared my cousin
& his pregnant girlfriend husband & wife by the power
vested in him by God & the City of New York

we all eat drink then move to the dining room
to find our place cards & I hope
I'm not sitting with my aunt who chants
the family book of marriage   who's still together   who's not
she asks me when you gonna get married
I say I'm too young just turned 21 everyone drinks
eats toasts the couple then dances to Kevin
& His Saints & Sinners   first the married couple
then the bride with her father the groom with his mother
the bride with her father-in-law the groom with his mother-in-law
the bride's father with the groom's mother the aunts with the uncles
they cut the cake the band's drunk the music faster they sing Elvis
his *hunka hunka Burning Love*

one grandmother does a spotlighted hula another the chachacha
everybody bunnyhops then hokey pokeys
a multi generational dancing line puts their right foot in right foot out
left hand in left hand out & shakes them all about
a cousin does a jig another a tarantella I ask a girl two years out
of high school to dance   after a few slow ones we step outside
her father right behind us

I walk away   catch a train
to a bar where a friend says all the writers
hang out   I try to sweet talk
an older woman a poet till she shakes her head says "no
you're too young   just a boy & already the light
in your eyes
is dimming"

genealogy   the lost grandfather

my great grandfather left Genoa & landed
alone
in Vermont
a marble cutter fleeing his own
civil war he quarried tomb-
stones for the Union dead   two years later
a wife & daughter came then two more
daughters were born & they moved
to the slums & gangs of New York's Five Points
where a friend told them the future
lie in fruits & vegetables   after fifteen more years & eight
more children they bought a brownstone
120th & Second   Italian Harlem

some names had changed
Cirella to Sarah
Achille to Archie
Francesco to Frank
by choice or census takers who chose
to baptize them "American"   my grandfather
married outside his tribe a Hungarian woman
they divorced   for a while my father lost his father
found him
when he & his two younger brothers knocked
on an apartment door   their father's new Spanish wife
pregnant with a fourth brother asked who they were
then asked them in

years later my father brought
a priest to bless his father's death
persuaded the priest to sign
a paper to open the ground
in the Catholic cemetery to this divorced
wayward son   bring him home

to rest with his family

when his wife read the death certificate
he was ten years older than the man
she thought she had married

a prayer for my Jewish grandfather

my mother buttons my white shirt
my grandfather has died tonight
is his wake I walk
quietly into the funeral parlor where everything
whispers the undertaker the family the taffeta
of my cousins' dresses we sit
in a silence that swallows
the light & one
by one rise
to kneel in front of his open coffin
I look for the cigar in his hands or the deck
of cards instead there is a rosary tied
around his fingers   this Jew (they whisper "he always wanted
to be a Catholic") left
his wife their five
children for my grandmother & her three sons
& in this moment of sorrow I stare
at his dark forehead it reminds me
of the table where Friday nights the family
gathered its wood rubbed deep
with whiskey & smoke & his long
journey from Hungary to this grim
room of flowers & I see
my eye reflected on his & lean back
taking my life
from his face I pray
may he have Dutch Masters & nights
of pinochle & Four Roses
may his hands forever
be free
of prayers

a visit to Calvary Cemetery

for my sister Joan

this is where the journey ends immigrants
who didn't lose
their names chiseled
into gravestones or above
the doors of family
mausoleums
we rise
thru ice
& snow to find
our family
& each turn in the cemetery road brings us closer
to my nephew his generation's first-
born laid out like the Infant
of Prague on the porch where we'd watch
black & white TV my father sports page sprawled
on his lap cigarette
smoldering between fingers lulled
to sleep by baseball's
droning announcers   closer
to my grandfather lulled
to death by work
or drink depending on who told
his story   closer
to my great grandfather perched
on his "throne" parrot at each shoulder
holding court till the growler of beer my father as a boy fetched
from the local tavern emptied
& was nailed to the kitchen table

we rise but the family
is lost
among others who came to plant
these stones
it doesn't matter   these stones don't hold
flesh only
the names
& as we walk the snow
gives way to our voices
& we raise the dead with stories
that drift
from our tongues like the blue
snow in childhood street-
lights the snow we'd pray would last all night
the snow that would close school
& open the day like the dead
open us to memory

a circle of women East Broadway 3 A.M. 1965

the big woman knows
to sit by the alley entrance
where a breeze might stir
& ease the heat

the youngest woman on the edge
of her chair watches
her shadow shrink
against the pavement when she speaks
how her husband squeezes
water
into stone

the thin woman bobs
from face
to face looking
to open scars to weave
a blanket of salt a woof
of pain a warp of sorrow

the old woman sighs
nods   bends
her ear to her heart

the big woman quietly rises
the air cool enough now
to go home open the bedroom window
lie naked on the sheets

the youngest woman shivers
says she'll stay a little longer
her husband almost gone
to work

the thin woman rests a hand
on the young woman's knee
she has much more
to tell her

the old woman's told all her stories
about her mother's journey in the stink
& sweat of steerage
about the pine coffins she saw as a girl
lined up on the sidewalk at the time
of the great influenza
about how her son had been a prisoner
of war in the same land
her parents had fled

this American life

for my grandmother

in spring my grandmother sewed dresses
three for my sisters three for my cousins
a skill she learned a young girl emerging
from steerage into New York's sweating
garment shops at the end of a grinding century
pins in mouth she draped the girls in organdy
taffeta chiffon & crinoline
marked & cut the cloth & for weeks worked
her needle by hand & treadle
Easter morning my sisters like little
pastel blue and yellow bubbles bobbed
down the hall to the floor length
mirror on the bathroom door twisting
their necks to see what others would see
walking behind them

one spring my grandmother took me
the only boy to buy my Easter clothes
she wore her flowered dress and sturdy shoes
the same way she dressed thirty years before in a photograph
my grandmother her three sons & her mother
on a picnic by the bay in the Bronx
at the end of the streetcar line
I wore my good shoes good pants good jacket
we rode the elevated through Queens
the conductor announcing each stop in an indecipherable mumble
the train squealing around curves
descending beneath the East River to Grand Central
then a double decked bus to Macy's where we ate
hot dogs sauerkraut a piece of apple pie   I was surprised
this year I wouldn't be a little man in a little gray suit
with a little fedora

she let me pick a chocolate sports coat flecks
of red woven into the fabric bluegray
pants brown loafers & a skinny maroon tie
a harbinger of my teenage quest for cool

I didn't know my grandmother
was a fatherless girl who sailed from poverty
to poverty & had three husbands
the first disappeared after a daughter's stillborn birth
the second my grandfather one of eleven children
his father an immigrant stone cutter who carved a life
out of New York's produce markets & moved his family uptown
maybe this son was her safe port   they divorced
because he lost his job or he drank
or joined a union or maybe her mother's constant
whispers "you can do better" cast her adrift   she ran
a boarding house cooked cleaned laundered
at night did piecework with her needles
at times fled one place for another when the rent came due
the third an older Jewish man from the neighborhood
had a steady business a wife & five children he left
for my grandmother & her three sons
he smoked cigars she cooked they played cards

when she died at 93 my mother sent a photograph
my grandmother in her flowered dress & sturdy shoes
smiling by the African violet I gave her when I left
the city for the West
& a note to her grandchildren
how she loved her sons
how our parents loved us
& we should honor them
how she prayed each night God might forgive
her youthful sins her sins of surviving
His gift of this
American life

Part II

It is dangerous to wander
backward, for all of a sudden
the past turns into a prison
                    —Pablo Neruda

memory

the juncos came back today one
in the red
maple hops branch
to branch while my daughters watch
the high
thin laughter of old
cartoons

at work the swallows have returned rattling
air with rapid
beeps
& dives
  beeps
    & dives
    this is one
kind of memory like the map the great
blue swims each year or the paths moon
flies from night
to morning
this is the big
memory that drowns
the dinosaurs in the dust of a pre-
nuclear nuclear
winter

my father remembers
not buying me a new bike after a childhood
accident I remember
my newspaper manager's ink bruised face close
to mine the stink of his stale cigar & a wail
spilling from the ambulance
like blood
& bent over a shot & beer
the driver who hit me a retired cop

forgets but wants to know
the score flickering
above the bar as the bartender wipes dust
from a row of unopened bottles
                    the jukebox skips
a beat so
skillfully no one notices anything
is missing
this is another kind of memory
what we create as the air
eats our lungs
food
for dreams images for the soul
to rise to & snap
like insects from the passing
waters

my mother sits in the common room
with a basket of family pictures in her lap a nest
of exiled memories her mind
a broken shell
we hand her our newest
born & her flesh remembers
how to rock
            to ease
                    a child
her cry chants through my mother's nodding head
like a prayer that's lost
its words a wind
that moves
nothing

Charles On Wheels

in late summer before the burning
of leaves in gutters when
the smell of hot tar popped
into air & nuns
who ordered the other three
seasons of our lives still
slept inside ivied convent walls & priests
were seen on faraway beaches in Aloha shirts & sneakers
Charles On Wheels his moustache trimmed
like Don Ameche's slowly
drove his black panel truck through
the streets a mobile fruit
& vegetable stand sweet
peaches apples
oranges tomatoes cool
green heads of lettuce all
laid out in rows like a flag
from a land beyond
our block where overalled
farmers joined hands
with their families & bowed
to the American cornucopia   Charles
On Wheels an envoy from a garden
more fruitful than Eden would give
the children fat
plums purple
teardrops of pleasure & we would
cry "Charles Charles the summer
is running from us   we've heard
the nuns' habits stirring" & Charles would honk
from the end of the block a black
sun at the end
      of the long
          last days
             of summer

the Knife Man

there was a mourning in his bell a heavy
clank of metal
on metal & in the houses a rush
to gather edges dulled
by the passing seasons
scissors
vegetable knives great
carving blades the children offered to the Knife Man
his skin stabbed taut by summer's heat
his face shadowed by the visor
of a gray cap
his eyes fell
back into his head like the eyes
of a starving wolf stalking
the deer with a worm
in its heart

the Knife Man spoke a language rough
as his knuckles skinned
on the sharpening
stone spun by his worn
boot on wooden
treadle
we didn't understand
the words but their sounds cracked
our bones
settled in their marrow

one day after he left
in the sanctuary
of my mother's kitchen I slid
my thumb down a sharpened
blade opening
flesh learning

the tongue
of wet fire I spoke
the Knife Man's language

the Good Humor Man

for e e cummings & Wallace Stevens

in twilight summer hours
beneath long arms
of oak or within
the hive of the mulberry bush its sour
berries sweet
appetizers to summer's cold feast we
waited for the white robed priest
of dessert to drive
his tabernacle of chocolate & toasted
almond down our street & we would chant "THE GOOD
HUMOR MAN IS COMING THE GOOD
HUMOR MAN IS COMING" & our bodies hummed
as we swarmed his truck impatient
for the small
white freezer doors to open
& reveal the steaming honey
of Dixie cup Creamsicle
& ice   when he slipped
the coins we begged
from our parents into the jangling
change maker hanging from his belt
& chose
one of us to sit in the open
cab & pull the bell cord
our hearts
pealed against our ribs the air
roared with his laughter

Bowne Park

winter is the first memory
sledding the slope above the pond the older kids head
first on
to the ice whining
under their weight & Stephen O Leary up to his knees
in mud
we bet him speed would carry the thin spots & fell
laughing as skates flashing he cracked fist
over fist through the ice

spring has no memory
probably the trees budded & leafed   the brown
lawns put on their green jackets
the pond shook off its ice
but we were busy
filling miter boxes with pennies nickels & dimes to feed
the starving children in China
forty days forty nights of Lent
no candy soda movies no
playing in Bowne Park until Jesus died
then rose

in summer we netted "sunnies" in pieces of screen suspended
from four corners by bakery string and baited with Krug's white bread
or cast the fresh water with salt water rods for the elusive
bass only Walter Keily or Johnny Robb had seen flash
at the deep
center
we'd feel it nibble & jerk to fix the hook but weeds
or a tangle of line was our catch
later we drifted from that water to the playground the big
swings where we wore our hair greased
back and filled our mouths with cigarettes
& curses & learned the taste

of cheap
wine a girl's tongue how to float perfect
smoke rings one
inside another

autumn is the last memory crazy
Sallie's Christ-
head tattoo bleeding under a broken street-
light the air roiling with a
capella harmonies our planet
tilted to the heat
of war
in Southeast Asia

how the brain works

for Rosalie Sorrels

Rosalie says love's a dog
named Dominic big tongue laps
her face after weeks
on the road   Dominic's a saint
Spanish Black Friar Dominican
founder who sent nuns from Ohio
into my childhood   Sister Ursula drilling
multiplication tables wood
pointer dangling
from her pinkie to crack
bad memory's knuckles
Sister Thecla cracking
John Sexton's head against the board chalk
halo billows from his hair

Dominic's my childhood barber Saturday
mornings new Marvel comics adjustable
chair paper collar fresh pin-
striped sheet draped around shoulders
neck shaved clean
by straight-edge stropped on leather
strap
manhood's
first
blood

how the brain works
love dog saint nun hair
floating to flowers of green
& white linoleum blood
on a sheet   love
is a dog

holy Manhattan

St Patrick's pricks the sky red with oil fumes & setting sun   the dead
cardinals' red hats/black ribbons float
from its eaves   banks
of votive candles shadow
the walls prayers   going up   in smoke

down-
town an old Italian leans
on a wrought iron railing   wine
easing tongue swaying
spirit like old
country night

"when we came   six adults five children
all in one room   a broken stove with crazy pipe
smoke leaking at every joint   a pile of rubbish
in the corner

I was blessed   a friend knew
a man looking
for a kid like me with smarts
& a strong back"

he cups
    a match
his face
    flickers
his eyes close
to its heat

full moon
slips through a broken window
the street chimes
with glass

the man who believes in nothing dies

the man who believes in nothing
makes a desperate sign of the cross he fears the end
of sex his last taste
of chocolate he holds
his final breath like an oyster
its precious pearl
the man who believes in nothing has a blue face
his temples throb
his hand pressed over his nose
& mouth he closes his eyes
the sacred number that's pulsed
his life shrinks
to a seed then blossoms a perfect
black
rose each
petal swollen
tense with beauty

the man who believes in nothing feels
a pin-point of fire sear
through the soft
spot of his skull a thin
blue finger enter
to pluck
his perfect rose

his breath steams
through the top
of his head a great tree unfolding
its arms to receive him

he feels his heart explode

road trip   a found photo

for Tom

you never had much luck
with cars the little Alfa
you owned for a week till your father woke you early
one Sunday to move it   he had to get his car
from the garage to drive
your mother and sisters to Mass   the Alfa wouldn't start
you rolled it to the street to park
it kept rolling you running
arms stretched through the driver's window
to hold the wheel   it left you
jumped the curb smacked
into a tree
or the Valiant you flipped on the New York
State Thruway   five teenage boys
a road trip   a week
camping drinking swimming naked in star-
crossed waters   a sudden
shout a swerve heels
over heads we crawled
out unhurt the Valiant not
so lucky

& here you are
another journey hood up
arms stretched finger-
tips printed with grease wide
smile
across your boyish face   your Falcon's
smoking grille
          grinning

Part III

I'd long felt these mountains and lakes
beckoning, and wouldn't have thought twice,
but my family and friends couldn't bear
talking about living apart. Then one lucky day
a strange feeling came over me, and I left...
　　　　　　　　　　　　　　　　—T'ao Ch'ien

riding the interstate

hawk
lights
an October
field
crow
saunters
black almost
blue
against the sky
the hills to the east are
vertebrae
of a thin man   face
submerged
in a river

like the smell of my grandfather's
room a year
after his death   the smell
of summer is not
yet a memory

my son is dreaming   cows
& sheep nose
the air

nothing arrives
nothing
is leaving

first language

for our Ancestors

I asked if English
was your second
language   you laughed said yes
first was breath   a year later we walked
moon pouring a path
through fallen cedars
& talked
how the Ancestors
moved
      across Earth
      to join us

the list

I make a list this morning
clean the gutters
store the hammock & sun
umbrella plant the garlic
under a blanket of newsprint
& straw to gather strength
beneath winter's insistent darkness
chop kindling split fir three years curing
under ragged green tarps
stack it by the house to burn the days
when snow drops an oak
across the power line

an angle of geese honks
& pulls me outside
a squirrel busily plants
acorns   another crazed
by winter's deep memory didn't see
the car taking the curve its driver
late for work   a blood-
headed vulture leaves a small dark
shadow on the pavement
in the garden a chill breeze bends
the cosmos taut then releases
a shower of seed burrows the earth

unhook the hoses
insulate the faucets
empty the water pots move them
where rain can't freeze
& crack them pick the last
fig

each evening
the sun setting farther
south behind the ridge
the list filling with un-
finished business

this for that

we empty the house to make room
for more
a continual exchange of goods
give away a bag of baby clothes
a teenager goes shopping
clean the refrigerator
relatives arrive
clear the table
fill the sink
an empty room needs
a chair to enjoy its emptiness
a haircut needs a new hat

I turned over the stillness of a dead possum
a galaxy of maggots glittered in its place
I blew up
a balloon for my daughter
this poem flew
into my mouth

anniversary

ten years since helicopters evacuated
America from Saigon's roof   Vietnam Vets spray
my neighborhood   stalk trees
with b.t. in a war against a natural
enemy   whir
of steel through air shakes
the earth my bed
shivers in the staccato
dawn my children
stand in the open
doorway excited

in Nicaragua Contras
spray farms with American bullets twist children
& grandparents into broken-limbed
sculptures plagiarized
from Wounded Knee Hiroshima
My Lai

starlings screech
at every pass

wedding at Mt. Pisgah

for Maia & Ryan

today there are family
friends strangers
on tiptoes gazing over one another's shoulders
rubbing a memory
into a stone in their pockets
there are promises   a kiss
by a river bearing day's end
it's a story they can tell everything
that makes their dream

but today the full moon begins
to disappear   open
your hands
you need no stone to hold
your moment   only
the changing light

November birth (Tewa moons)

for Achille

rain fell all
that April   the snort
& rustle of horses
among trees
in moon when leaves
open

in fall my son fell
into my hands
each breath a gift
in the season of harvest

gathering moon
         cradled
his body

crepuscule

for Fia & Gina

drifts of late summer clouds glimmer
salmon & violet   mammoth sunflowers
sway their shaggy heads glint
in the gloaming a slow blues winds
through an open window   a baby cries
tired unpracticed her mother tips
her breast to the child's
hunger

in the dark a small tongue curls latches
to a tender
nipple

adoption

Growth Report
---Chang Ji Fang

Chang Ji Fang, female, was born on March 30, 2006. Her date of birth was determined by the doctor. She was picked up in Lihuaxincun Food Market of Changzhou City on Oct. 11, 2006. She was sent into our institute by Chaoyangqiao Police Station of Changzhou City.

After she came into the institute, Ji Fang received a check-up and the results showed: cleft lip of both sides, complete cleft palate of both sides. In spite of that, her physical and mental developments were normal. We named her Chang Ji Fang.

The origin of her name:
Chang: Changzhou City
Ji: the second character of orphans' names who were adopted in 2006
Fang: typical female's name

Ji Fang has cleft lip and palate. When she first came into the institute, she was easy to spit out formula. She was very weak. Caregivers looked after her very carefully and patiently. With their efforts, Ji Fang became plump and seemed healthy. She was sent to De'an Hospital, Changzhou City to receive cleft lip repair surgery on Jan. 25, 2007. She recovered well after the surgery.

Ji Fang entered the nursling nutrition program on Oct. 15, 2006. She is held and cared by "grandma" there. She developed close relationship with "grandma". She is held by "grandma" to the playroom every day. She is learning all kinds of motions and exercise with grandma's help. Now she can crawl around to look for her favorite toys and playmates. She can turn over independently and sit playing with toys. She is also able to stand up by supporting the railing of her crib.

Ji Fang is an easy-going and quiet girl. She is not afraid of strangers and smile at person. She likes playing with person.

Changzhou Children's Welfare Institute
July 18, 2007

a "quiet girl" fierce eyes
she climbs the door frame   spread
eagle   the backyard tree without fear
she rides her horse standing
upright in the stirrups checks
her posture in the arena mirror
teases her brother six years older
three feet taller   tells her grandfather
he has a "weird" eye it wanders

this girl who swings fearlessly
rung to rung on the playground
this girl who tells her mother to wait all day
outside her classroom door till school
is over

climbing Mt. Pisgah

it takes time to learn
to walk this way
to match
breath to step   step
to slope

at the top   back
against rock   solitary
soul drifts
in/out of sleep
bamboo flute leans
against knee   breeze
singing through it

below river
flows at each point
a deep
stillness

morning walk

just beyond the memory
bench where the owl-
eyed man sometimes stops
to stretch & limber where the trail curves
& edges the road   two
vultures spread
their wings & rise into a shiver
of cottonwoods above
a gravel bedded creek

a young buck lies in a patch of spent
camas petals scattered ribs picked
clean newly antlered head
& hind quarters still
intact   I hesitate
then move on   vultures patient
creek chanting
young buck dreaming
his way home

spring fever

in this month of the green
apostle
before beebuzz and pollen
when horny toms
fan tails & gobble
                    gobble after flirty hens
when the day's promise
is the promise of work the need
to hold the wild
in hand to prune
mow dig haul lift push
pull   on this morning
my boots
& gloves gather
the last
heat from night's
dying
fire
a flicker half-
heartedly chases
towhees from the suet   squirrels chatter
through down-
pours
the dog groans
as she dreams
by the door
& like Jesus the morning after
a good Friday I lie
quietly
waiting
for the stone to roll
from my eyes
& I plan
how I'll move

a rose   maybe plant
an oak in the north field
a maple
in the east   how I might
dig a small pond   stack
a stone wall build
a rain house where
my wife & I sip
tea around a tight fire & watch
in winter
storms gather
then flow from the hills shaking
the bamboo sometimes
bowing
them to the ground   I plan
how I will
keep up with this land as it stirs
sprouts erupts
into an unruly throng
their song setting trees
to blossom their dance luring
even a bloodied
Jesus to rise
from death & walk
one last time
this earth in glorious riot

hand me my gloves
my fiery boots
I
am ready

struggling into spring

I

snow took our plum down this spring
sat in the tree's white blossoming branches
till it sighed then tumbled
its roots wrenched
from the sodden hillside pointed
at the sky   astonished

2

a doe is curled at the foot
of the oak by the coil
of rusted barbed wire no sign
of violence   I cover her
with dirt & winter
browned fronds cut
this week from beds
of emerging iris

3

from New York our daughter sends
words through the air "spent 10
hrs in L & D last night
baby's fine still kickin' salsa
in the womb   diggin' Coltrane ballads
when she sleeps"

mowing

I know the time
for first mowing
I've learned
the subtle swale
how different grasses respond
to the blades how low
to duck beneath the oak to save
my scalp how to balance
my weight to cut sidehill
how to brake to descend the steep
slope   every year something new
an unfamiliar grass a volunteer
oak emerging from a blackberry
tangle or what
is new are small
places my dog is first to find as she grows
old the warm
in early spring the cool
in summer
& as I watch
the hawks the crows the jays   the flicker
who comes the last two days
to feast on ants in the rotting
wood bounding the garden beds my body
slows becomes one
more changing
constant
in this place
I call
home

weeding

My dream is to walk out all alone into a lovely
morning maybe stop to pull weeds in the garden,
maybe climb East Ridge and chant, settling into
my breath, or sit writing poems beside a clear stream…
                                    —T'ao Ch'ien

I sat in the backyard sullen
stabbing dirt while friends
who lived in apartments rode their Schwinns
Raleighs & Western Flyers joyously
to the airstrip to watch
Piper Cubs glide
in over Flushing Bay propellers
thumping   tires
bouncing on the dirt runway
then they raced to Sy's Luncheonette
to sit on red stools & sip
vanilla egg creams while I cursed
the sun my face hot
sweaty my hands
torn by angry
roses why
did I
have to live
in a house
shovel snow all winter   in summer
mow the lawn help my father
put up screens & worst
of all   WEED   who cared
if there was grass
in the garden dandelions
in the lawn
I was losing
my boyhood

now in another century in another land
I sit for hours in my garden probing
the ground loosening
the soil around a weed's deep
root to ease
it unbroken from the earth
I know the one that pops
out with a quick pull
the one I can grab
by the handful
& I know how some can try
to hide inside a respectable
sounding name like Bristly
Hawksbeard or a sweet one
like Wild Morning Glory
while they sink their feet deep
into the clay beneath me

& I know there are ways
in autumn to ease
this work thru spring
& summer   but by then
my ardor slows   drunk
on ripe tomatoes fresh
basil a lazy
red wine

besides I have nowhere
to go because no one
makes an egg cream
like Sy anymore
& that airstrip is long
long gone
to seed

the meadow

survey stakes bleed the meadow
where our daughter walked
first loves & light
carried shadows of her changing
body
where wanderers chance
on an old fence line a broken gate a path
to the winter pond hidden
in blackberry thickets

maybe we can confuse them pull
the stakes slip wild roses
in their stead
call the hornets come
build your humming nests here
swarm those who would try
to tame you

then we can walk
our grandchildren through the thicket
show them how things come
& go the pond the broken gate
the fence someone thought once
would be
forever

the chair

a neighbor gleans
tomatoes purple plums apples
from our yard   tosses
her dog a windfall

I watch from the chair by the window
the chair my daughter calls
"Tom's chair" my best friend's
chair from his backroom apartment the chair
his caregiver gave him to comfort
his disappearing body in spring's first days the chair
we brought home to hold
his absence

cicadae

for Spike and Fang Fang

seventeen years under this ground they've sipped
rain siphoned through blades of grass
suckled roots of black walnuts maples a single magnolia
a million in this acre

last night they climbed through the dark
tiny hills of crumbled dirt
up tree trunks & the sides
of an old red garage
shed their root/yellow
carapace & emerged pale
& white   a large red
eye on either side of their head

their wings wet shriveled
unfold translucent in the morning
& lift their now florescent
green bodies in
to the flickering canopy   a chorus
of male sopranos   (one's highest note
could break
a person's drum if sung
by her ear) swells
& fills the light   at noon
drenches the air becomes a desperate
carnival of maracas a frenzy
of rattles bursting
into a joyous scattering
of seed

six weeks for the eggs to hatch
for the blind nymphs
to form then fall
from the trees   for the earth
to take them in

& begin
again

anthem

five crows row the sky
join three others hovering
above a stand of fir ferociously
cawing   one
then another
drops into the upper branches
till a hawk screams out
catches a draft
& ascends
a jay riding its ear

for a moment they're an avian
flag   the hawk
a sun orbited from above
& below by eight black
feathered planets the jay a small
blue star busily fluttering against a blue
field they fill with wild
cacophony a fierce
anthem

      o say
did you see
that brave jay
eight steady crows
that hawk soaring   its red
tail in day's true
light

gleaming

learning to paint

for Kathy Hoy

in Basic English my students fight
nouns verbs the structure
of a sentence
a forty year old woman who can bead
intricate ancestral designs is near
tears
a thirty year old man who's lost
his job   who knows the grammar
of machines shrugs
& holds his head

I tell them my story
of learning to paint
how I hate my teacher's ease
with the brush how her trees look
like trees her bamboo like eloquent
characters on a Chinese
scroll

how in my hand the brush is a cat
going its own way imperious
in its disdain I try
to think how Lao Tsu thinks
bend like the willow to my frustration
but my willow looks like that cat
& I
want to smash
the ink
against the wall & shout
THAT IS ART

we laugh   our heads nodding
                    like leaves
                        in a slow
                            black
                            drip
of rain

fighting sleep

for Ren

every night our daughter fights sleep
first she takes the wobbly journey
through her crinkled picture books pointing
& crying out "**HORSE**"
"**COW**" "**CHICKEN**" then she sings full-voiced
over & over the tale of the "teensy
weensy spider"
then she talks talks talks

what holds her here
her dreams so sweet we'd fall
into them in an instant

maybe it's just
her great joy
in the wandering
gather
of language

explaining the mysteries Siena Italy

bring me the head
of Caterina di Siena
& they do
& her finger & the scourge
she used to whip the Devil
from the flesh she pledged
to Jesus at the age of seven

my daughter is silent
then asks how can Jesus have
so many women
I point to the gold
wedding bands on the fingers
of two passing nuns & begin
to explain but she says I know
he's like Dracula one bite
they're his wives
forever

after reading *The Tao of Physics*

my wife enjoys baking in the pink twilight
our youngest daughter sleeps when she never closes
her eyes before midnight
the TV silent
the older children read

& I read about subatomic physics how these moments
of rest are bits
of matter named grace
& beauty   how everything moves
everything

& I think how Donny Moore the relief
pitcher threw a single
                        hanging
curve that kept his team out
of the World
Series
then shot his wife & killed
himself

& I climb to the roof
adjust the antenna & pray
for divine interference

dog

eyes black
stars
pulled
shut
from within
ear now
& then turning to the horn
of some
great
ship sinking
into its own
reflection

she lies
in the grease
spot
of a garage whose doors
fade
green & open
onto a drive-
way of weeds
& broken brick

all her life she sleeps
in a perfect
circle

Part IV

> Or maybe a boy who ran away from home
> comes home today – today when the fog lifts
> across the river, and he forgets his whole life –
> the hard times, the hunger, the betrayal of trust –
> as he stops at a corner and drinks the morning air.
> It's worth it, coming home, though you're not the same.
> —Cesare Pavese

solo

Billy was a saxophone played
Bronx tenements subways Times Square Bleeker the Bowery
a man on the sidewalk dead tattooed with words
Billy played the Flushing local   his grandfather
asleep beside him smelled of Old Spice & cigars
in the summer Billy watched him hoe & water helped him
till it became a job

Billy's father sang Sinatra Caruso his mother played
piano   Vinnie Caine a cop who hated the poor for not
feeling privileged sang first tenor his daughter beautiful
Billy pursued in the seventh grade   he hadn't read
Plato his perfect
                          idea
                          of love

Billy was a saxophone played straight
pool bowled
the third floor alleys 70 year old "boys" setting pins for pints
of wine   Billy played the jukebox
in the pizza place Sunday afternoon dances in the Catholic
hospital the girl from Brooklyn an hour
on the Jamaica line for 15
minutes in the cold

Billy's father took him to Calvary   Billy played
the names Achille Giorgio marble cutter vegetable man
Billy was a saxophone played his first time she
was kind Billy took her to White Castle after
put her in a cab

Billy played fire   buildings famous for a moment then ash
& steel bone   Billy played conga timbales record
store loudspeakers rats scuttling through garbage

trucks picked up once a week   Billy played children cold
turkey shivering at birth

Billy played women till their lips wore thin   when they left
his heart
shrank
to a fist

Billy was a saxophone played wind-
blown newspapers unfolding from the dead
like tattooed skins

Billy played the high
flying salvation psalms the low
down damnation blues & he knew
all the changes

& Billy knew he'd made the nine First Fridays
so he was guaranteed a priest to hear
his sins & bless his horn
when it was time
to blow
his last solo

tough guy in moonlight

in 7th grade he sat
last row last seat
head on desk asleep
Sister Cleopha slapped
his ear he laughed her face red
hand
trembling   on the playground no one
looked him in the eye afraid
to wake his hands
two furious stones tearing
holes in God's light

seven years later I poured
drinks in a seaside bar I'd learned
to know a little
about a lot
could talk to the toughest guy
who'd be in the Series where
to find parts for a '63
Impala how
he knocked that "fucking
bartender from the dive down the street
flat out"   I gave him free drinks
to cool
the bad drunks

now he leans on a thick
stick worn
smooth by scarred
fingers & muscled weight & shuffles
in the shadows to a slow
blues as the woman the nuns
warned the girls they'd become
if they danced with the tough guy takes
his empty hand

OK

last night I photographed New York's rivers
of street light as a dozen men slept on the sanctuary
of a cathedral's wet concrete steps
farther on a young man lying
on the sidewalk in a black
suit drunk cheek pressed against shining pavement wallet open
on the street beside him
slowly raised his right arm bent the tip
of his index finger to the tip
of his thumb pointed his middle ring & pinkie fingers to the sky
to say I'm OK I'm not
drowning

riding the 6

catch the 6 at 51st & Lex
along the train's length doors open
some passengers stride out some
stumble backward onto the platform the car
so crowded when they boarded they could never
turn around   we slip into the space a big fast-food counterman
vacates as he heads to his midday shift
grab a bar for balance   plant our feet
to lean into curves rock forward
then back as the train starts
& stops

half way down the car a young man
torn sneakers ragged pants an old red t-shirt
stares at his left hand a clenched
fist dyed purple a dried snakeskin hangs
across his throat   facing him another
young man creased khakis starched
white shirt wrings his hands left
over right right over left gaze fixed he sits
upright
elbows pinned to ribs to keep
space between his skin
& the tired weight of the hotel
housekeeper on one side the elevator
mechanic on the other

by the door three young Chinese
women chat & giggle
the pitch & rise & fall of their voices turning
the sound "ma" to "horse" or "mother"
"hemp" or "scold"   two children peek
from behind their mother's legs   nervous
she watches her husband study

the subway map by the window   they're lost
going down when they want to go up-
town "next stop 42nd Street
change to the 4 the 5 the 7"   three
more stops to Union Square its green market
where a bearded man talks
to the bearded dragon on his shoulder
we buy cheese bread a few upstate apples
to fuel our journey back
through the wormhole beneath
these city streets

50 years ago I rode this line five days a week
a stack of books beneath my aching arm
algebra history religion Latin French & Greek a skinny
kid in love with the polyphony
of tongues the synchronous
sway of bodies flesh
to flesh the tired
faces flashing in the windows of the passing
uptown express like frames
from a film noir
the third rail's steady spark marked
this synaptic map now unfolding stop
by stop from an un-
bound
sheaf of memories

gentrified

in memory of 157th Street
Flushing, Queens, New York

no one on the street
no Jimmy Murphy playing
with fire behind Gregory's garage   no
silent James
McGrath rocking
insistently on the porch outside his bedroom lined
with shelves
of National Geographics   no
pompadoured Eddie Hoppe trying
to seduce my sister by the mulberry bush   no
Julianne Fenchak whispering
to Rosemary Lawrence
on the stoop across the street bookbag
at her feet   long
hair burning   no
vigilant Virgin
Mary in the grotto
in the Quinns' front yard
no coal man opening
the chute to the Wiley's
blackened bin
no rag man leading
his horse cart mournfully
crying "rags rags"
no bread man knocking
at the front door
no Charles On Wheels trolling
with his black truck
of fruits & vegetables
no milk man delivering
two quarts each

topped with an inch
of cream to the milk box
on the kitchen steps
no knife man sparking
the families' knives on his spinning
stone
no ice cream man jinglejangling
his eucharistic bells children
crowding the street to receive
his communion of Dixie Cup
& creamsicle   no
punchball game the asphalt
chalked with bases
& foul & home run lines   no
Ruboni brothers no Sclafanis no
Paulie Hoppe no
Tommy Finch   no
radios chanting off
the innings of Yankees
Giants my beloved Dodgers   no
Ernie Beban & my father beer
in hand steaming
clams on the cinderblock barbeque
built to span exactly
the property line between them   no twilight
settling onto tarred
pavement scarred
lawns no
hide n seek no
all ie all ie umph free
no punk
smoke to ward off
summer's first
mosquitoes
no
late night
whispers under blue
streetlight   no

secret whistle to call me down
from my midnight
bedroom window to sit
on the curb
& listen

no one
on this street   only
immaculate lawns sculpted
bushes carefully pruned
trees each
yard magazine
perfect posts a small
sign a polite
petition that the City
of New York declare
this landscape
forever
historic

on the sad train

on the sad train to Poughkeepsie rain
streaked windows frame
the Hudson's gray bank
its abandoned factories
its old towns where old
men hunch over drinks in sour taverns
while their wives in old houses mop
the footprints of absent
children from their kitchen floors

the black footings of the Tappan Zee Bridge
shadow the pocked waters the ferryman
once plied   its wide
deck reaching through
a nimbus of fog to the river's
far bank

the woman sitting behind me
has a familiar voice filled
with dank sorrow & complaint
she talks about two babies
dead in their cribs
a husband who left the house
each weekday for a year
to a job that didn't
exist

"last stop   Poughkeepsie"

I hear the woman drag her suitcase
from the rack above her seat
watch her pass
through the doors her back curved
to shed the downpour

"Poughkeepsie" in the First People's tongue
"u – puku – ipi – sing"
"the reed covered lodge
by the little water place" the sacred spring
the end of the line   sodden
with rain chant & the sad
sad songs of trains

coda

for Tom

today we go to Strawberry Hill to drink
red wine eat smoked salmon mussels good bread
float some flowers in the sea
poppy daisy columbine the colors of spring
which greeted you
as you entered our home

are you still rolling
in these waves singing
with the whales roaring in winter storms whispering
songs in full moonlight   you're here
in memory conversation a dream I tried
to touch you so alive
dead in a single moment

I go to music venues
look at their calendars for your name
I pass your apartment will you walk
down those crooked steps today
I lay on the sand your face in my eyes
you singing your last breath

you picked this spot
for your ash & bits of bone
where water falls
from cliff to sea where tides
smooth a field of stones & sun
fills them with warmth

I carry you home
my brother a stone
in my pocket

Iraq memorial

we are a field
of white
flags   we
surrendered   flesh
to earth   bones
to memory's
river   we are
a torrent buried
beneath boots who lost
the light
step   the way
to dance

we were surprised
by freedom

the day John Coltrane died (cont.)

on the forty-seventh anniversary
of John Coltrane's death
Eric Garner stopped a fight
on the Staten Island street corner
where he sometimes sold
single untaxed cigarettes
two police officers arrived
& announced their intent to arrest him
he objected   kept moving his hands
to avoid being cuffed
three more came
the five surrounded him
one put his forearm across Garner's throat
the others pulled him to the ground
Garner cried "I can't breathe"
one knelt on his back
another pressed Garner's face into the pavement
eleven more times Garner repeated
"I can't breathe"

on the day John Coltrane died
graced by his family's presence
his wife Alice Turiya says his last breath
was "beautiful" maybe he'd found
that more beautiful sound he always
was seeking

on that same date
forty-seven years later
a block from his home
& family Eric Garner died

in the arms of five
New York City policemen
his last words his last breath

I can't breathe

Trane songs

for John Coltrane

         the long
drink of roots *After*
the Rain *Naima* his first wife's
tranquil name the quick
              descent
                of *Giant*
                   Steps the slow
heartbreaks *Every*
Time We Say
Goodbye   the weeping
lights of *Central Park*
West   the deep
chant of *A Love*
Supreme the keen-
ing horns of *India* *AfroBlue's*
blue ancestral waltz *First Meditations* *Meditations*
OM   Earth's moan
as she receives four
young girls murdered
in a church in *Alabama*   *Dear Lord*

the hymn I played that day
my mother died

cremation

for my mother

bone bursts
into flame
the flesh I come from
is the ash she's becoming

in my childhood's last
days   leaves
fell   I burned
them along the curb   smoke
filled my eyes

I'm blind
with remembering
torn open
by fire

coffee

grade school mornings I woke
to my mother downstairs
at the mottled gray kitchen table alone
with her coffee   waiting
for my sisters & me to come down
pour our cereal into plastic
bowls   drown it
with milk & sugar   our father
asleep until we left

I don't know if my mother drank
another cup before he came down
or maybe a third with him
I loved its aroma but not
its taste

the last time I sat alone
with my mother she was drinking a cup
in the kitchen of the apartment
my parents moved to the summer I left
& they sold the house
& gave away my childhood
trains comics & shoeboxes
of baseball cards

she had talked to the young parish priest
he assured her I would come back
to the Holy Mother the Church   I was silent
waiting for her to change
the subject tell me
who had died who had married
how she & my father were moving to Florida
when my youngest sister left
for college

I didn't visit often
avoiding arguments with my father
about religion Vietnam Civil Rights
my father a self-made lawyer built his case
with classic logic I countered with stories
songs & poems the volume rising
till silenced by our angry shouts

my mother coming to me after whispering
your father loves you

I never went back to that mother the Church
I moved & found faith in a small piece of land
the songlines of its trees
stones plants soil its birds fluttering
back & forth between tangles of rosemary
& hanging seed feeders   the deer grazing
on fallen crab apples
the squirrels burying acorns
in winter's tired gardens

now in my 70's I take a pen a notebook & drive
to a downtown bakery a few times
a week   order a pastry
something savory sometimes sweet
& a cup of coffee brewed fresh splashed
with cream to ease my tongue give me time
to unknot the bitterness   understand the lonely
quietude of its taste

confession

at dawn I took my glove
& ball & opened the front
door to a scraggly patch
of lawn where a squirrel sat
an acorn between its front feet
that I saw for the first time were little
hands that now raised
the acorn to its mouth to eat
& I wondered if I could hit him
with the ball threw it hard
& fast blood splattered from his eye
a perfect pitch

I walked cautiously to him proud
but scared he was dead
I was alone the neighborhood quiet
I picked the ball up tried
to wipe the blood off on the grass
it seeped into the rawhide I hid it
in my glove the blood staining
the leather I had worked for weeks
at night oiling it with linseed oil
then cradling the ball in the center
& wrapping a leather thong tight around
the glove to create a perfect pocket

I turned the squirrel over with a stick
the other eye milky & still
the bread man would be coming soon
& the paper boy   I dug a shallow
hole with my hands beneath an evergreen bush
lifted the squirrel by its tail & curled it in
then covered it with dirt then rocks
then fallen needles

Notes

"learning to box": The phrase, "The Sweet Science" comes from five volumes of boxing articles titled *Boxiana* written by Pierce Egan from 1813 to 1825. In his writing he often refers to boxing as the "Sweet Science of Bruising," a phrase that acknowledges boxers as both methodical and tough. From 1951 to 1955, AJ Libeling wrote a series of boxing articles for *The New Yorker*. He published the collection under the title, *The Sweet Science* as a tribute to Egan.

"solo": The "nine First Fridays" in the last stanza refers to the Roman Catholic Church's promise that believers who attend Mass on the First Fridays of nine consecutive months are assured that a priest will be present prior to their imminent deaths to hear their last confessions and to administer last rites.

Acknowledgments

Grateful acknowledgement is made to the publications in which the following poems first appeared or are forthcoming. Some of the poems have been revised since their original publication.

Black Bear Review: "the man who believes in nothing dies"
Blast Furnace: "how the brain works"
Burning Word: "tough guy in moonlight"
Cascadia Review: "anthem" and "the meadow"
Chiron Review: "learning to dance," "Brooklyn girls," "learning to box," "the wedding reception," "after reading *The Tao of Physics*," "this for that," and "on a sad train"
Clackamas Literary Review: "spring fever"
The College Moment: "climbing Mt. Pisgah" and "Iraq memorial"
Denali: "the Knife Man"
Fireweed: "a visit to Calvary Cemetery"
The Mas Tequila Review: "riding the 6," "Bowne Park," and "explaining the mysteries"
New York Dreaming: "gentrified"
Pacifica: "a prayer for my Jewish grandfather"
The Paterson Literary Review: "this American life"
Poetic Space: "anniversary"
The Poet's Billow Literary Gallery: " cicadae"
Raven Chronicles: "morning walk"
Seattle Review: "moving pianos"
Silverfish Review: "Charles On Wheels"
Spike 2: "holy Manhattan"
williwaw journal: "coffee"
Willow Springs: "dog"
Windfall: "the list" and "mowing"
Wisconsin Review: "memory"

"solo" was reprinted in *The Anthology of Eugene Writers #1*. Northwest Review Books.

"the day John Coltrane died" appeared in *Take a Stand: Art Against Hate*. A Raven Chronicles Press Anthology.

Earlier versions of "moving pianos" & "solo" were included in a limited edition book of poems, *midnight the blues*, from sight | for | sight books.

Earlier versions of "riding the interstate" and "November birth" were included in a chapbook, *sparking the rain*, from Silverfish Review Press.

The complete song, *hard times*, can be heard on "Fast Folk a Community of Singers & Songwriters" on Smithsonian Folkways Recordings.

Thank you:

to my wife, Lynn, for her love & steadfast belief in these poems

to my children for all the good times we've shared

to my grandchildren for giving me the privilege of being their grandfather

to Joy Harjo, who workshopped this book with me, sharing her time & her great ear

to Father Sky/Mother Earth for teaching me a new language

to all the students I taught over forty years for the gifts of your interest & effort

& special thanks to Rodger Moody, a good friend & a master editor

& to Ralph Salisbury, whose friendship & guidance set me on this long journey of learning to make words sing

May Peace Prevail

About the Author

Frank Rossini was born in 1946 in the Flushing section of New York City. He attended Catholic schools for 16 years, graduating from Fordham University with a B.A in English. He began a 43-year career in education as a student teacher in Roxbury, Massachusetts & a student in Harvard University's Graduate School of Education. He also began writing song lyrics with a boyhood friend, Tom Intondi, a singer/songwriter on the Greenwich Village folk music scene. Along the way, he met Tom Weatherly, the author of *Mau Mau American Cantos,* who encouraged him to write poetry. In 1972, he moved to Eugene, Oregon where he taught in a program for young migrant farmworkers at the University of Oregon & completed a Masters of Education & an MFA in Creative Writing. From 1980 to 2010, he was an instructor at Lane Community College, working with adult learners. He has written & published poetry in various journals over the past fifty years. Silverfish Review published a chapbook of his poems, *sparking the rain,* in 1979. In 2012, sight | for | sight books published a limited edition book of his poems, *midnight the blues,* which focuses on his long love of jazz that began with a spiritual awakening at midnight on January 1, 1968 while listening to John Coltrane's *A Love Supreme* for the first time. He lives with his wife, Lynn Nakamura, & their dog, Camas, on a small piece of land on the edge of Eugene, where he writes, listens to jazz, & tends a "wild garden."

The interior text and display type were set in Adobe Jenson, a faithful electronic version of the 1470 roman face of Nicolas Jenson. Jenson was a Frenchman employed as the mintmaster at Tours. Legend has it that he was sent to Mainz in 1458 by Charles VII to learn the new art of printing in the shop of Gutenberg, and import it to France. But he never returned, appearing in Venice in 1468; there his first roman types appeared, in his edition of Eusebius. He moved to Rome at the invitation of Pope Sixtus IV, where he died in 1480.

Type historian Daniel Berkeley Updike praises the Jenson Roman for "its readability, its mellowness of form, and the evenness of color in mass." Updike concludes, "Jenson's roman types have been the accepted models for roman letters ever since he made them, and, repeatedly copied in our own day, have never been equalled."

The front cover text was set in Arno Pro. Named after the Florentine river, which runs through the heart of the Italian Renaissance, Arno draws on the warmth and readability of early humanist typefaces of the 15th and 16th centuries. Though inspired by the past, Arno is distinctly contemporary in both appearance and function. Designed by Robert Slimbach, Arno is a meticulously crafted face in the tradition of early Venetian and Aldine book typefaces. The back cover text was set in Minion Pro. Designed by Robert Slimbach in 1990, Minion is inspired by classical, old style typefaces of the late Renaissance, a period of elegant, beautiful, and highly readable type designs. Created primarily for text setting, Minion combines the aesthetic and functional qualities that make text type highly readable.

Cover design by Valerie Brewster, Scribe Typography
Text design by Rodger Moody and Connie Kudura, ProtoType
Printed on acid-free paper by McNaughton & Gunn, Inc.